A Gift For: _____

From: _____

Copyright © 2017 Hallmark Licensing, LLC

Published by Hallmark Gift Books,
a division of Hallmark Cards, Inc.,
Kansas City, MO 64141
Visit us on the Web at Hallmark.com.

Editorial Director: Delia Berrigan
Editor: Kim Schworm Acosta
Art Director: Chris Opheim
Designer/Production Designer: Dan Horton

ISBN: 978-1-63059-850-1
XKT1396

Made in China
0717

Rex Snows the Way to Grandma's

Written by Diana Manning   Illustrated by Mike Esberg

The Icesnickle family was all loaded up
with goodies and gifts and their lovable pup.
They were headed to Grandma's, for Christmas was near,
and they traveled the long road to see her each year.

But after they'd gone many miles in the snow,

they came to a stop with a "What?" and a "Whoa!"

"There's snow way to get there!" the Icesnickles feared.

No Christmas at Grandma's? Now that would be weird!

Oh, being at Grandma's was always such fun—
she made every Christmas a wonderful one!
She cooked and she knitted, like some grandmas do,
but always took time for a snowball fight, too!

All of a sudden, Rex sniffed at the air—
he knew how to find them another way there.
His keen canine sniffer had picked up a scent,
and off through the snow-covered mountains he went!

His family was puzzled but followed him still
'til they came to a lake by the side of a hill.
Two fun, friendly fellows were fishing away—
that seafood aroma had led Rex astray.

"OK," sighed his family. "I guess we'll keep looking."

And once again, Rex thought he smelled Grandma's cooking . . .

They followed their pup and found Eddie the Yeti
preparing a big batch of Christmas spaghetti!
"You're welcome to join us," said Eddie. "Please stay!"
But the Icesnickles knew they should be on their way.

Rex ran ahead, smelling something divine—
where in the world would they end up THIS time?

They came to a campsite where acorns were roasting
and crashed a big party some squirrels were hosting.

Rex started chasing the squirrels here and there
'til once more he sniffed a new smell in the air.
This time he knew it was Grandma's for sure!
That gingerbread baking just HAD to be her!

He finally reached Grandma's and barked his "Hello"
then realized his family was back in the snow!

He looked at the mantel and thought of a plan—

he snatched up a stocking and suddenly ran.

He found his whole family back where they had been,

and boy, were they happy to see him again!

"What's this?" wondered Dad, at the yarn he had brought.

"Just what could that pup have been up to?" he thought.

But Rex only barked at the way up ahead,

'til Snow Belle was certain of what he had said.

"He wants us to follow this yarn he's unraveled!"

So off through the snowdrifts to Grandma's they traveled.

The yarn led them right up to Grandma's front door—
she hugged them all tight; then she hugged them some more.
"Good boy!" they told Rex as they patted his head.
"You helped us reach Grandma's by Christmas!" they said.

Despite all the detours they had to go through,

just being together was worth it they knew.

Since family, no matter how far or how near,

is what puts the merry in Christmas each year.

And amid all the hugging and munching and talking,

Grandma got busy on Rex's new stocking.

'Cause she knew that Santa was certain to leave

more dog treats than ever on THIS Christmas Eve!

If this chilly adventure warmed your heart,
or if perhaps you just liked the art,
we would love to hear from you.

Please write a review at Hallmark.com,
e-mail us at booknotes@hallmark.com,
or send your comments to:

Hallmark Book Feedback
P.O. Box 419034
Mail Drop 100
Kansas City, MO 64141